JEAN-PHILIPPE ARROU-VIGNOD ✱ OLIVIER TALLEC

ZERO TO TEN

Who's that knocking at the door?
Oh my goodness, Rita's friend is here!

'I warn you, Whatsit, don't spoil everything.
Just for once I've got a friend coming.'

Alfie lives in a flat across the road. A very small
flat, with only a balcony for a garden.

'Whatever have you brought?' cries Rita.
'My TV of course. Can't I watch it?'

It will be fun having a friend round!
Rita has planned all sorts of things to do: going on
the swings, skipping competitions, blind man's
buff…

'I'm bored!' says Alfie.
'When are we having tea?'

Tea? Rita has other plans: a spot of gardening with her friends in the sunshine.
But what's that peeping out of the watering can?

'That's Monster, my hamster,'
says Alfie.

Oh no, what a disaster!
This little furry monster has gobbled up all
the daisies and nibbled the geraniums!

'What about making a witch's brew?'
suggests Rita.
'You mix up bits of grass, some mud,
some camomile leaves…'

'Are you mad?' says Alfie.
'I'm not a girl, you know!'

Rita is getting rather cross with Alfie. What's
the use of a friend who doesn't want to play?
At teatime they all sit round the table sulking.

'Having a good time?' asks Mum.

If Alfie's going to be a spoilsport, decides Rita, tough!
I'll go and play with Whatsit.

But where is he?

He's with Alfie...

It's good fun having a friend round, thinks
Whatsit.
You can play marbles, football, and lots of
other boy games.

And there's nothing more
fun than a real wrestling
match!
'Oi, what's the matter
with you two?' shouts
Rita.

But they aren't listening.
Because girls just don't understand.

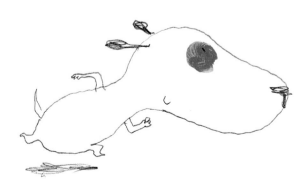

And when you're worn out, you can
relax with a game of cards.

'You're all cheating!' says Rita.
'Fetch us some crisps and leave the
men to battle it out,' says Alfie.

It's the end of the afternoon. Time for Alfie
to go home.

'Hey, you can't leave yet,' cries Rita. 'We've
got to tidy up!'
'No time,' says Alfie. 'Coming, Monster?
There's a match on TV we can watch.'

Rita is exhausted. It's hard work having a friend like
Alfie round.

'You know what, Whatsit? *You* are my best friend.
Next Saturday, I promise it will just be the two of
us. We can play whatever you want.'

'OK, but only if you let me win…'
'Whatsit, you cheeky monkey! Come on, give
me a big hug.'

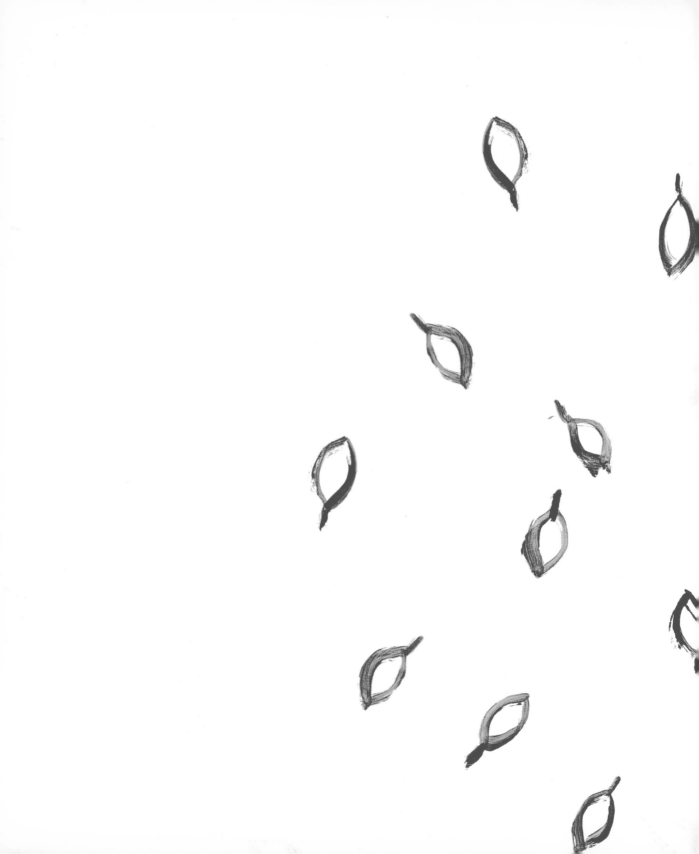

First published in Great Britain in 2008
by Zero To Ten Limited
2A Portman Mansions, Chiltern Street,
London W1U 6NR

This edition © 2008 Zero To Ten Limited
© Gallimard Jeunesse 2007

First published in France in 2007 as
L'invite de Rita et Machin

British Library Cataloguing in Publication Data:
Arrou-Vignod, Jean-Philippe, 1958-
Rita and Whatsit's new friend
1. Rita (Fictitious character : Arrou-Vignod) - Juvenile
fiction 2. Whatsit (Fictitious character) - Juvenile
fiction 3. Children's stories
I. Title II. Tallec, Olivier
843.9'14[J]

ISBN 9781840895247

Printed in China